KB263614

The Home of the Heart

A Poetry Collection by Kim, Cho Hye

김초혜 영문시집

The
Home of the
Heart 마음의 집

Translated by
Kim, Tae Kyun & Kim, Yoon Shik

There is a saying that translation is an act of betrayal, yet without translation, the radiant exchange of the world's cultures could never have taken place.

It is through that creative power that my poems now have the opportunity to meet readers around the world who understand English.

It brings me great joy that Dr. Kim, Tae Kyun, a distinguished physician of profound literary sensibility, and his son, Mr. Kim, Yoon Shik have joined as co-translators of this work. The fact that they are father and son lends this collaboration an even deeper warmth and significance.

I extend my heartfelt gratitude to them both.

Fall 2025
Kim, Cho Hye

■ 영문판 시집을 내며

번역은 반역이라는 말도 있지만 번역이 없었다면 이 찬란한 세계문화교류는 이루어지지 않았을 것이다.

그 창조적 힘에 실려 이번에 내 시가 영어를 이해하는 세계의 독자들과 만나는 기회를 얻게 되었다.

문학의 이해와 조예가 깊은 저명한 외과의사인 김태균 선생님과 김윤식 선생까지 공역자로 참여하게 되어 큰 기쁨을 얻게 되었다. 더구나 두 분이 부자지간이라 그 의미가 더욱 정답다.

두 분께 고마운 마음을 표한다.

2025년 가을

김초혜

I am always thinking.

Because I believe thought itself is creation.

Perhaps the infinite power within thought

is what poetry truly is.

If I go even a single day without reading a book

or reflecting on poetry,

I feel as though I age all at once.

So I read, and I write.

This year marks the 60th anniversary of my life

in poetry.

Spring 2024

Kim, Cho Hye

늘 생각한다.
생각이 창조라고 여기기 때문이다.
생각 속에 있는 무한능력이
시가 아닐까.
하루라도 책을 읽지 않거나
시를 생각하지 않으면
부쩍 늙는 것 같다.
그래서 읽고 쓴다.
올해로 시업 60주년이다.

2024년 봄

김초혜

Part 1

Part 3

Part 4

Part 6

Part 1

Eons

Avalokiteshvara Bodhisattva

Even three thousand prostrations are

but a single lump

of burning tears

영겁

관세음보살

삼천배도

한 덩이

뜨거운 눈물이다

People

Where there is a great mountain,

the smaller ones cannot be seen

but if there are only low hills,

even small mountains are visible

Great mountains,

small mountains,

low hills—

all these mountains

are mountains I love

사람

큰 산이 있는 곳에서는
낮은 산이 보이지 않지만
동산만 있으면
낮은 산도 보인다
큰 산
낮은 산
동산
그 산들은 모두
내가 사랑하는 산이다

It Is Good

Sorrow is good
Suffering is good
Pain is good
Even agony is good

All of it is good

as long as it is not an eternal farewell

좋다

슬픔도 좋다
괴로움도 좋다
아픔도 좋다
고통도 좋다

모두 좋다

영이별만 아니라면

Thinking of Home

From the kimchi soup

I had for dinner,

a thousand strands of memory

made me put down my spoon

고향 생각

저녁에 먹은

김칫국에서

천 갈래의 기억이

수저를 놓게 했다

Time

24

Even the painful things

that seemed they would never be forgotten

even after a million, ten million eons

were all carried away by time

시간

백만겁 백천만겁이 지나도
잊혀지지 않을 것 같던
아픈 일도
시간에 모두 실려 가더라

Mouth

If you meet
someone with ten mouths,
then you,
even with just one mouth,
should close it

Even one is too many

입

입이 열 개인
사람을 만나거든
그대는
한 개인 입도
닫아버려라

한 개도 많다

Practice

Do not eat until you're full
When you still want more,
put down your spoon
Words I've heard since childhood
from my mother
I never knew
there was practice in them

수행

배부를 때까지 먹지 마라
더 먹고 싶을 때
수저를 놓아라
어린 시절부터 들어온
어머니 말씀
그 안에 수행이
담겨 있는 줄을

Contentment

Still you say it is not enough
You have food to eat,
a place to sleep,
and quietly,
unseen by anyone,
flower seeds are blooming
toward you
Still,
what are you lacking?

만족

아직도 부족해
먹을 것이 있고
잠잘 곳이 있고
그리고
아무도 모르게
그대를 향해
꽃씨가 벙글고 있는데
아직도
무엇이 부족해

Next Life

It remains

in the hearts

of those

who are left behind

내생

남은

사람들의

가슴에

있다

Finger-pointing

They say glory and disgrace
are vain and fleeting,
but the finger-pointing
behind one's back
can bring a person
to their knees
When the numbers grow—
a thousand, ten thousand—
even without illness,
one will collapse in pain

손가락질

영욕은 부질없고
속절없다 하지만
뒤에서 하는
손가락질이
그 사람을
쓰러뜨린다
천 명 만 명
그 숫자가 늘어나면
병이 없어도
앓아눕는다

Disciple

Poor,

kind,

and diligent—

that's why

I like you

제자

가난하고
착하고
부지런하고

그래서

나는 네가 좋다

Enlightenment

If enlightenment means

freeing oneself

from joy, anger, sorrow, and pleasure, and

the five desires and seven emotions,

then enlightenment

is too cruel

a reverence

깨달음

희로애락과
오욕칠정에서
벗어나는 것이
깨달음이라면
깨달음은
너무 잔인한
우러름이다

Name

The most beautiful name
in this world
is Spring
And there is another name
just like Spring

But that is a secret

이름

이 세상에서
가장 아름다운 이름은
봄입니다
봄과 같은 이름이
또 있지요

그건 비밀입니다

Blemish

Even a small blemish
is still a blemish

If a single fly
falls into a finished dish,
it must be thrown away

If even one strand of hair
is found in a delicious soup,
the whole soup must be discarded

흠

작은 흠도 흠이다

다 된 음식에
파리 한 마리 들어가도
버려야 하고

맛있는 국에
머리카락 한 올만 들어가도
국을 버려야 한다

Nagging

Even a deaf person,

if told more than three times,

will grow weary

and run away

How much more so, then,

for someone

with keen hearing?

잔소리

귀먹은 사람도
세 번 이상 말하면
질려서
도망가는데
하물며
귀 밝은 사람이랴

Avatamsaka Sutra

You who have blinded my eyes

so I cannot see ahead,

do you say that

if I only open my heart,

being blind

is nothing at all?

Do you tell me to behold you

while deaf,

and while mute?

화엄경

내 눈을 멀게 해
앞을 볼 수 없게
만드신 이여
마음만 열면
눈먼 것은
일도 아니란 듯이
귀먹은 채로
벙어리가 된 채로
그대를 친견하라 하십니까

There Is None

To the great monk
I had long served,
I asked,

"Is there a next life?"

After a long silence,

"There is none."

없다

평소 섬기던
큰스님께

내세가 있습니까

긴 침묵 끝에

없다

Part 2

Woljeongsa Temple

In a place so deeply, endlessly green,
there resides Venerable Jeongnyeom—
"Only when stillness is allowed to settle
can it truly be called stillness",—
his teaching says

With palms together,
I receive it

월정사

푸르고 푸른 곳
거기 정념 스님 계시어
―고요가 고이게 해야
비로소 고요라는 가르침―

합장으로
받습니다

Sharing

If you have ten,

do not give just one

If you have only two,

give one

And to someone

who truly needs it,

even if you have only one,

gladly

give it

나눔

네게 열 개 있어야
한 개 주지 말고
두 개 있거든
하나 주어라
꼭 필요한 사람에게는
한 개밖에 없어도
기꺼이
그것을 주어라

There Is Light

Darkness
where not even an inch ahead
can be seen

Yet within the darkness,
there is no darkness

빛이 있다

한 치 앞을
볼 수 없는 어둠

어둠 속에는
어둠이 없다

Hometown Moon

Whenever
and wherever I see it
the brightest moon
in this world
is the hometown moon
of my childhood

고향달

언제
어디서 보아도
이 세상에서
제일로 밝은 달은
어린 시절
고향달이오

Mother

Even the blind
recognize their child
and even the mute's words
are understood by the mother

Even an elephant
can recognize its lost calf
by scent
after twelve long years

어머니

맹인도
자식은 알아보고
농아의 말도
어미는 알아듣는다

코끼리도 잃어버렸던
새끼를
12년이 지난 후에도
냄새로 알아낸다

When the Magnolia Blooms

The magnolia

that bloomed last spring

has blossomed white again

in the front yard this year

You, whom I thought

had long gone,

come back like this

every year

목련이 필 때

지난해 봄에 핀
목련이
올해도 앞뜰에
하얗게 피었습니다
아주 간 줄 알았던
그대가
해마다 이렇게
오시는군요

In Life

When the moon rests on the mountain

when the first snow falls

when the cornelian cherry blossoms

a faint fever stirs

I remember the time

when we promised to look upon them together

whether living apart

or living together

삶 속에서

달이 산에 걸리고
첫눈이 내리고
산수유가 피어나면
미열이 난다
헤어져 살아도
같이 바라보자던
그때가 생각난다

Hill after Hill

Here comes my ten-year-old self, as if dreaming
Here comes my twenty-year-old self, drunk on
the new spring
Here comes my thirty-year-old self, exhausted
from fatigue
Here comes my forty-year-old self, crying inside
but smiling outwardly
Here comes my fifty-year-old self, smiling
outwardly
Here comes my sixty-year-old self, neither crying
nor smiling
Here comes my seventy-year-old self, with
calmness and composure as companions
My eighty-year-old self goes, smiling

고개 고개 넘어

열 살의 내가 꿈을 꾸듯 오는구나
스무 살의 내가 새봄에 취해서 오는구나
서른 살의 내가 피곤에 지쳐 오는구나
마흔 살의 내가 속으로 울고 겉으로는 웃고 오는구나
쉰 살의 내가 웃고 오는구나
예순 살의 내가 울지도 않고 웃지도 않고 오는구나
일흔 살의 내가 고요함과 평정심을 친구 삼아 오는구나
여든 살의 내가 웃으며 가고 있구나

Rice Pot

I am nothing more

than a fifty-kilogram

rice pot

When warm and full,

I spare no glance at my side

I'm just a rice pot

Yet to fill this mere

fifty-kilogram rice pot,

I have struggled

through an entire lifetime

밥통

나는 50킬로그램짜리
밥통이올시다
등 따뜻하고 배부르면
곁에 눈도 주지 않는
밥통에 불과합니다
겨우 50킬로그램짜리
밥통을 채우기 위해
한세상 허덕였습니다

With Only One

With one leg

you cannot walk far

With one pillar

you cannot build a house

Alone

you cannot even fight

협치

다리 하나로
먼 길을 갈 수 없고
기둥 하나로는
집을 지을 수 없고
혼자서는
싸울 수도 없다

The Ways of the World

I will not go

to his son's wedding

But isn't he your closest friend?

Ah, I no longer have

a child left to marry off

세상인심

나는 그의 아들
결혼식에 안 가겠네
아니 둘도 없는 친구 아닌가
아, 나는 이제 결혼시킬
자식이 없거든

Hometown

Parents are a hometown
Any place where you can recall
your parents and siblings
is a hometown

Memories, too, are a hometown

고향

부모는 고향이다
부모 형제를
떠올릴 수 있는 곳은
어디나 고향이다

추억도 고향이다

Slander

A quiet
whispered word
can make a roar
more frightening
than thunder and lightning

중상모략

조용하게
소곤거리는 귀엣말이
천둥 벼락보다
더 무서운
굉음을 낼 수 있다

Sometimes, Sometimes

Even when snow-laden branches
grow heavy,
they just quietly
shake themselves off sometimes
Yes,
so it was with our lives too
Carrying heavy burdens,
sometimes, sometimes,
we lived only looking up
at the sky

가끔씩 가끔씩

눈 쌓인 나뭇가지가
무거워도
말도 없이
가끔씩 몸만 터는구나
그래
우리네 인생도 그랬지
무거운 짐을 지고서
가끔씩 가끔씩
하늘만 보며 살았지

A Good Day

You may come before the plum blossoms bloom
You may come when the plum blossoms bloom
You may come after the plum blossoms have
fallen
For longing neither ceases
nor withers away

좋은 날

매화가 피기 전에 와도 좋고
매화가 필 때 와도 좋고
매화가 지고 나서 와도 좋다
그리움은
지칠 줄도 모르고
시들지도 않으니까

Love

Strength may overcome

a mother

But love

cannot overcome

a mother

Give your love

to your child

who is full of strength

사랑

기운은 어머니를
이길 수 있지만
사랑은 어머니를
이길 수 없다
네 사랑은
기운 좋은
네 자식에게 주어라

Darkness

Alone,

I cannot venture out

on a night path

But with two,

I can walk it

And with three,

we walk singing

Going together,

strength comes

without gathering strength

어둠

혼자서는 밤길에
나설 수 없지만
둘이서는 갈 수 있고
셋이서 가면
노래를 부르며 간다
같이 가면
힘을 모으지 않아도
힘이 난다

To My Friend

The cold wind
makes flowers fall

The gentle wind
makes flowers bloom

친구에게

찬바람은
꽃을 지게 하고

순한 바람은
꽃을 피우더라

Part 3

Spinach Soup

Mom, why do you
only eat the broth?

I just
like the broth

I thought
she really did

시금칫국

엄마는 왜
국물만 먹어

나는 국물이
좋아

그런 줄만
알았다

Rebirth

An ancient pine,

hundreds of years old,

withered away in pain,

and the following year,

it bore hundreds of pinecones

and departed

The next year,

where the pine had left,

countless young pine shoots

sprang forth

환생

수백 년 된 소나무가
시름시름 앓더니
그다음 해에
수백 개의 솔방울을 낳아놓고
그리고 소나무는 떠났다
다음 해에 소나무가
떠나간 자리에
소나무의 어린싹이
수없이 솟아올랐다

On a Fading Day

94

I thought I had planted peonies
and waited for peonies to bloom
but they never did
so I folded up my spring dreams

저무는 날에

모란을 심은 줄 알고
모란을 기다렸는데
모란은 피지 않아
봄꿈을 접었습니다

A Lifetime

Fearing my shameful self
might be seen by others,
I spent a lifetime
covering my own eyes
I thought
if I covered them,
all would be hidden

일생

부끄러운 모습을
남에게 들킬까 두려워
일생 내 눈만
가리고 살았습니다
가리면 가려지는 줄
알았습니다

Blossoms

Chusa wore holes
into ten inkstones
He ground the ink
again and again
until holes were through

Surely, the Inkstone, ink, and brush
must have worn out his whole body

The true script standing with dignity,
the semi-cursive script walking with graceful
pride,
and the cursive script racing
like a horse with its mane flying—
they were all blossoms,
blossom upon blossom

꽃송이

추사는 열 개의 벼루에
구멍을 냈다
구멍이 뚫리도록
먹을 갈고 또 갈았다

벼루와 먹과 붓이
온몸을 닳게 했으리라

기품 있게 서 있는 진서와
도도하게 걷는 것 같은 행서며
말이 갈기를 날리며 달리듯 하는
초서는
그대로 꽃송이 꽃송이였다

In a Fluster

With my right hand,

I reached for the worldly life

With my left hand,

I reached for a life beyond it

In such a fluster,

I ended up

grasping nothing at all

허둥지둥

오른손으로는
세속을
왼손으로는
탈속을
허둥지둥 아무것도
잡지 못했지요

Longing

In every shimmer of haze,
the days gone by
bloom again

Even if it is a pain
that cuts through my heart,
I long for it

Even that indifferent breeze
that stayed for a while and left,
I long for it still

그리움

아지랑이마다
지난 일들이
피어난다

그것이 가슴을 에는
고통일지라도
그립다

머물다가 간
무심한 그 바람도
그립다

To My Poetry

You live within me

Within me,
You hold
joy, anger, sorrow, pleasure,
the five desires and seven emotions

You wait
for the day to hatch

나의 시에게

내 안에 산다

내 안에서
희로애락, 오욕칠정
품고 있다

부화될 날을 기다린다

Moonlit Night

It was bright outside,
so I opened the window

The moon was shining

It was
your greeting

달밤

밖이 환해서
창문을 열어보니

달이 밝았소

그대의
안부였구려

Great Inheritance

The worn book
that grandfather read
was read and aged by his son
The book his son read
was read by his son,
wearing down its pages
And the book that son read
was read by his son,
and again by his son,
and again by his son—

Read,
and read,
and read

위대한 상속

할아버지가 읽던
때 묻은 책을
아들이 읽어 낡게 하고
그 아들이 읽은 책을
그의 아들이 읽어
책장을 헐게 만들고
또 그 아들이 읽던 책을
그 아들이 읽고
또 그 아들이 읽고

읽고 읽고 읽고

To My Son

I, your mother,

even in death cannot truly die,

even in decay cannot truly decay

For you,

even in the night of death,

I would remain awake

Even if my body

were to vanish,

my love for you

would remain as it is,

dissolved within you

아들에게

에미는
죽어서도 죽지 못하고
썩어서도 썩지 못하고
너를 위해서라면
죽음의 밤에도
깨어 있을 것 같다
육신이 사라진다 해도
너에 대한 사랑은
그대로 남아
네 안에 녹아 있을 것이다

I Don't Know

A mountain is a mountain,

so why do you say

you do not know a mountain?

Water is water,

so why do you say

you do not know water?

A person is a person,

so why do you say

you cannot see a person?

Let go of a mountain,

let go of water,

let go of a person

Is it because

then all can be seen?

모른다

산이 산인데
왜 산을
모른다 하십니까
물이 물인데
왜 물을
모른다 하십니까
사람이 사람인데
왜 사람이
안 보인다 하십니까

산도 내려놓고
물도 내려놓고
사람도 내려놓아야

다 보이기 때문인가요

Conviction

They call it conviction,
but it sounds like self-righteousness

They gently call it
a thought,

but it appears as stubbornness

소신

소신이라고 말하지만
독선으로 들리고

생각이라고
순하게 말은 하지만

고집으로 보인다

Parents and Children

A child

is the pain of a parent

A parent

is the burden of a child

부모와 자식

자식은
부모의 아픔인데

부모는
자식의 짐이다

A Young Spring Day

What am I to do

when, helplessly,

the flowers bloom in full?

After a single gust of wind,

the mountain before me

has turned into a mountain of blossoms

In the flower-colored breeze

blowing over the hill,

as I catch my breath,

you, long forgotten,

suddenly return

어린 봄날

어찌하라고
속절도 없이
꽃은 만발하는가
한파람 건듯 불고 나니
앞산은 꽃산이 되었고
고개 넘어 불어오는
꽃빛 바람에
숨을 몰아쉬면
잊혀졌던 그대가
문득 오시는구나

Sweet Trick

The promise to help
when I have plenty
is a sly way
of saying I won't help

Abundance,
when someone reaches out for it,
quickly
hides away

달콤한 꼼수

여유 있을 때
돕겠다는 약속은
돕지 않겠다는
꼼수다

여유는 누가
손을 내밀면
아주 빠르게
숨는다

On a Snowy Day

Snow is falling

The one in my heart,
you—

have once again
taken a step toward me

눈 오는 날에

눈이 내린다

마음에 있는
그대가

또
발걸음을 했구나

Diligence

One who walks every day

can easily walk

ten thousand miles

No matter

how well one runs,

one cannot reach

ten thousand miles by running

근면

매일 걷는 사람은
만리도
쉽게 걷는다

아무리
뜀박질을 잘해도
뛰어서
만리를 갈 수 없다

Part 4

Who Is It

They say
the fish was mocked
for swallowing the hook
But in truth,
who is it
that swallows
things far worse
than a hook
day after day?

누구인가요

물고기가
낚싯바늘을 삼킨다고
비웃었다지요
정작
매일매일 낚싯바늘보다
더한 것을
삼킨 것은
누구인가요

Oh, Human

Even beasts stop eating

when they have had enough,

but humans,

the more they eat,

the more they crave,

until they devour

themselves to ruin

사람아

짐승도 먹을 만치 먹으면
먹는 것을 멈추는데
사람은 먹을수록
더 먹으려 한다
자기 자신을
무너뜨릴 때까지
먹는다

Repentance

They say
even stepping on
a single sprout
is a sin

Then how many flowers
have I trampled
all this time?

참회

새싹 한 잎만
밟아도
죄업이라 하는데

나는 그동안
얼마나 많은
꽃을 밟았나

Life in This World

It is a winding,
ever-turning road

a path layered
fold upon fold

The road tells us
to live in the present,
yet we stepped onto a path
that kills the present
in order to live

세상살이

굽이굽이 굽이쳐
흐르는 길이고

겹겹이 첩첩한
길이다

길은 현재를 살라고 하지만
우리는 현재를 죽이는 길로
들어서서 살았습니다

Labor Suppression

It takes one person

leaving this world

for the long-endured

crater to erupt,

setting fire

to the hearts

of ten thousand people

노동 탄압

한 사람이
세상을 달리해야
참고 참던
분화구가 터져서
만 사람의 가슴에
불을 지르게 된다

Forgiveness

When I think
that every cause
was my fault,
forgiveness comes easily

But I forgive
only myself

용서

모든 원인은
내가 잘못이라고
생각하면
금방 용서가 된다

나는 나만
용서한다

The Classics

This friend has stayed by my side for a lifetime,

always speaking with me in warm harmony

Though an old friend

from a hundred, even a thousand years ago,

I feel neither the weight of years

nor any distance of generations

It is a friend sent as a blessing

Had I not conversed with these friends,

I would have had no way

to learn what is high and low in this world,

and what is near and far

But learning from these friends,

knowledge itself becomes a joy

고전

이 벗은 평생 곁에 있어
언제나 나와 정답게 소통한다
백년 전 천년 전쯤의
나이가 많은 벗인데도
연륜을 느끼거나 세대 차이를
전혀 느끼지 못한다
축복으로 온 친구다
이 벗들과 교류가 없었다면
세상의 높고 낮음과
멀고 가까운 것을
배울 도리가 없었을 텐데
그 벗들에게 배우고 익히니
앎이 저절로 즐거움이다

Books

Rather than practicing

by meeting a foolish person

filled with selfishness,

spending time quietly with you

is far more soothing

Even when I live alone in stillness,

I do not feel lonely,

for with just a turn of my head,

a reach of my hand,

hundreds and thousands of friends

warmly take my hand

책

이기심으로 가득 찬
어리석은 사람을 만나
수행하는 것보다
그대와 오손도손 지내는 것이
훨씬 편안하다오
한적하게 홀로 지내도
적막하지 않은 것은
고개만 돌려
손을 뻗으면
수백 수천의 벗이
정다이 손을 잡아주기 때문이오

On a Moonlit Night

When the round, bright moon
extinguishes all the darkness
of this world,
will even the melody of love,
that secretly swallowed
a lump of tears,
grow bright?
Will it shine
on the soul weeping
inside the hollow shell of desire?
Will it illuminate
even the hidden corners,
the bending paths unseen,
the high mountains and the low ones alike?
When we step beyond pain,
can everything, everything,
become bright?

달밤에

둥그런 밝은 달이
이 세상의 어둠을
모두 꺼버리면
남몰래 울음덩이를 삼키던
사랑의 곡조도 밝아질까요
욕망의 헛껍데기 속에서
울고 있는 영혼까지
밝게 비춰줄까요
휘어져 안 보이는 구석까지
높은 산도 낮은 산도
밝게 비추일까요
고통을 딛고 넘어서면
모두 모두
밝아질 수 있을까요

To Stand Alone

— To Jo, Jae Myeon

Now is the time to pound your fist

against the world with all your strength

If you wish to walk the path you desire,

blood must flow from your fist

Each time you feel pain from the bleeding,

the door of the world will open little by little

And when you finally have a fist

that bleeds no longer from pounding,

then, at last, you will stand alone

홀로 서다

—조재면에게

지금은 세상을 향해

힘껏 주먹을 두드려야 할 때다

네가 가고 싶은 길을 가려면

주먹에서 피가 흘러야 한다

흐르는 피를 아파할 때마다

세상의 문이 조금씩 열릴 것이다

두드려도 피가 나지 않는

주먹을 가지게 되었을 때

드디어 홀로 서게 될 것이다

Weary Joy

You,

the one who set

the fire of joy within me—

It all burned to ash

and died away,

yet you kindle it again

with that same hardship

What am I to do?

This endlessly hungry,

weary joy—

how can you tell me

to fold it away,

again and again?

고단한 기쁨

그대
나에게 기쁨의 불을
놓으신 이여
다 타서 재도
사그라들었는데
다시 불태우는
그 고난
어찌하란 말입니까
못내 허기진
고단한 기쁨
어떻게
접고 또 접으라
하시는 겁니까

Mother's Love

I know well what you mean
when you tell me
to let go of everything
and live in ease
But even if I were
to let go of the whole world,
I cannot let go of you—
this mother's love
is nothing but aching sorrow

모정

모두 놓아버리고
편하게 지내라는
네 말을 모르는 것 아니다만
세상을 다 놓아버린대도
너만은 못 놓는
모정은 애닯기만 하구나

Money and Women

No matter how swift

or clever a fish may be,

once it bites the bait,

its fate is surely

a sudden, tragic death

돈과 여자

물고기가 아무리

민활하다 해도

미끼에 걸려들면

반드시 비명횡사한다

Life's Journey

Waves-

before one

even fades away,

another wave

comes rushing in

relentlessly,

breathlessly

인생길

파도는
그 하나가
스러지기도 전에
또 다른 파도가
쉬임 없이
숨 가쁘게 몰려온다

Yes, Yes

The child monk statue

sent by artist Lee, Sang Ho from Gwangju

keeps nodding all day

and taps his moktak

whenever there is light

Even to the rambling sophistry without reason,

Yes, yes, you are right

Even to the vile acts that evade the truth,

Yes, yes, you are right

Yes, yes, only you are right

Always, you are right

The child monk is on my side

And I am on the child monk's side, too

그래, 그래

광주 이상호 화백이 보내준
동자승은
빛만 있으면
하루 종일 고개를 끄덕이며
목탁을 두드린다
경우 없이 늘어놓는 궤변에도
그래 그래 네가 옳다
진실을 비켜서는 비열함에도
그래 그래 네가 옳다
그래 그래 너만 옳다
항시 네가 옳다
동자승은 내 편이다
나도 동자승 편이다

At Dusk

I thought
there were still
a hundred thousand miles
left on this road,

but before I knew it,
the light had dimmed—
it is already dusk

해 질 녘에

갈 길이
십만 리나 넘게
남았는 줄 알았는데

어느덧
어둑어둑
해 질 녘이구나

Migratory Bird

Are you a butterfly,

that you flit

from this flower

to that one?

Is it because each flower

has a different scent,

and you wish to wander

again and again,

intoxicated

by each fragrance?

But just as the colors

of the flowers differ,

can the fact their scents differ

truly be your excuse?

철새

그대가 나비랴
어찌 이 꽃에서
저 꽃으로
자리바꿈을 하느냐
꽃마다 향내가 달라서
거듭거듭
다른 꽃으로 옮겨 다니며
그 향내에
취하고 싶다는 것이냐
꽃빛깔도 다르듯이
꽃내가 다르다는 것으로
변명이 될까

Autumn Leaves

Is it

because they wished,

even just once,

to become flowers

that the autumn leaves

turn red?

If even a stone

wants to become a flower,

is it then

used as a Buddha?

Did I too

wish to be a flower

and so love

this fleeting world?

단풍

단풍은
한 번만이라도
꽃이 되고 싶어
빨갛게 물든 것인가
돌도 꽃이 되고 싶으면
부처로 쓰임 하는가
나도 꽃이고 싶어
한세상과 사랑을 했을까

Part 5

Poet

A poet must hear
the sound of a heart
even from a taxidermied deer,
must feel the midday heat
from a cicada's egg,
the cuckoo's cry
from a cuckoo's egg,
and the autumn silence
from a wildflower, and
a poet must awaken
to the truths of the universe

시인

시인은 박제된 사슴에서도
심장의 소리를 들어야 하고
매미 알에서 한낮의 더위를
뻐꾸기 알에서도 뻐꾸기 울음소리를
기러기 알에서도 가을날의 적막함을
풀꽃에서는 우주의 이치를
깨달아야 한다고

The Sound of Stillness

Leaning into the dawn,
I listen to the sound
of wind and trees meeting,
the sound of a lotus bud
gently blooming
Within the stillness,
I hear a sound
that blossoms
into deeper stillness

고요 소리

새벽에 기대어 듣는
바람과 나무가
만나는 소리
연꽃의 봉오리가
벙글어 오는 소리
고요 속에서
고요로 피어나는
소리를 듣는다

Such a Person

When bitten by a viper,
there is a cure,
but when bitten by a person,
there is none

The scar lasts long

그런 사람

독사에게 물리면
약이 있지만
사람에게 물리면
약이 없다

그 흉터는 오래간다

Family

If just one

gets angry,

everyone gets angry

If just one person

is in pain,

everyone hurts

Even when

we are apart,

we live

entwined together

가족

한 사람만
화를 내도
모두가 화가 난다
한 사람만
아파도
모두가 아프다
우리는
따로 있어도
얽혀 사는 것이다

To You

It's hard, isn't it?
Yes, it must be hard
But even so,
you're doing all right
There are so many
who can't manage that much
Though they may look
comfortable outside,
if you look inside,
there isn't a single person
without hardship
They say our lives
hold as many worries
as the countless stars
in the sky
Yes, you've endured well

그대에게

힘들지, 그래 힘들 거야
그래도 그만하면
괜찮아
세상에 그만큼도
못한 사람이
얼마나 많은데
겉보기에는 편해 보여도
그 속내를 보면
힘들지 않은 사람은
하나도 없어
하늘에 잔별만큼
우리네 인생살이
근심도 많다 하잖아
그래, 잘 견뎠어

Human Nature

In front, they call you elder brother,
behind, they speak down to you

In front, they smile,
behind, they sneer

인심

앞에서는 형님이라 하고
뒤에서는 하대한다

앞에서는 웃고
뒤에서는 비웃는다

Spring Will Come

Have you ever seen grass
fear the frost?
If you fear hardship,
you are not truly young
Just as flowers fall easily,
hardship too will pass
When spring is warm,
winter feels even colder
If you endure the cold season well,
spring will come

봄은 온다

풀이 서리를
두려워하는 것을 보았는가
고생을 두려워하면
젊음이 아니다
꽃이 쉽게 지듯이
고생도 그리 지나간다
봄이 따뜻하면
겨울이 더 춥듯이
추운 시절을
잘 견디면
봄이 올 것이다

Between Father and Son

Go east, my son

I'm on my way now

Are you still going?

I'll turn west

so I can head east

부자지간

동쪽으로 가거라 아들아
지금 가고 있어요
아직도 가고 있느냐
서쪽으로 돌아서
동쪽으로 가려고요

Black Melancholy

I was only

caught by time,

but never

truly

caught time myself

검은 우울

나는 세월에게

낚이기만 했지

정작

세월을

낚지 못했다

Distance between Parents and Children

The distance that opened
since bodies separated
is mercilessly widened
by time
Only after eternal farewell
are they drawn close again
The providence
of life and death—
no one can truly know

부모 자식

몸이 나뉘고부터
벌어진 거리는
세월이 인정사정없이
벌려놓았다가
영이별 후에나
다시 가깝게 붙여놓는
삶과 죽음의 차이
이 섭리는
아무도 모를 테지요

A Modern Fable

In this world,

there are many people

who seeped into the bodies

of dogs or cats

and became human

요즘 우화

세상에는
개나 고양이의
몸속으로 스며들어
인간이 된
사람들이 많다

Spring Again

Even in the deep of winter

they respond to each other

Even before spring arrives

it is already spring

다시 봄에

한겨울에도

서로 화답하니

봄도 오기 전

벌써 봄이다

Dream, My Friend

O youth,

create a pill from air,

one a day

enough to fill the stomach

Create a pill

that devours

the ultrafine dust in the air

꿈꾸라, 그대

젊음이여
공기로 알약을 만들어
하루 한 알만 먹어도
배가 부른
식품을 만들어라
초미세 먼지를 잡아먹는
알약을 만들어라

Logic

It's, a tiger
No, it's a leopard

It's, a goat
No, it's a sheep, I tell you

It's, a house
It's a residence

It's a person
No, it's a human being

논리

호랑이 입니다
아니요 표범입니다

염소 입니다
아니, 양이라니까요

집 입니다
주택입니다

사람입니다
아니 인간입니다

Just Because You're Old

Just because you're old

doesn't mean you're wise

Just because you're old

doesn't mean you write good poetry

Just because you're old

doesn't mean you're free of greed

Just because you're old

doesn't mean you have good character

나이 많다고

나이 많다고
지혜로운 것도 아니고
나이 많다고
시를 잘 쓰는 것도 아니고
나이 많다고
욕심이 없는 것도 아니고
나이 많다고
인품이 있는 것도 아니라네

In the Empty Sky

Believing that
eternal time existed,
I walked and walked
a long, distant road
to come this far—
only to find
this was not the road
I truly wished to reach

빈 하늘에

영겁의 세월이
있는 줄 알고
멀고 먼 길을
걸어서 걸어서
여기까지 왔으나
그 길은
내가 다 닿고자 한
길이 아니었다니

Inheritance

When my son just entered elementary school,
there was something I passed down early
The ownerless—
mountains, rivers, the sea,
and the sun, the moon, and the stars—
I said, "I leave them all to you."
At first he blinked his eyes
with a puzzled look,
and much later he said,

"Then the sound of water and the wind—
Mom, you can have them"

The sun that rises each day,
the moon that waxes and wanes each month,
green mountains, crimson hills,
rivers flowing without stopping,

the sea, neither shrinking nor overflowing
After that, whenever he saw mountains,
even when gazing at the autumn sky,
or looking out the window as snow fell,
he would say,
"Mom, you can have all this too"

And so, a whole world quietly passed by

상속

아들이 초등학교에 막 입학했을 때
일찌감치 상속한 것이 있었다
주인 없는
산과 강, 바다 그리고 해, 달, 별
모두 너에게 상속할게
처음에는 눈을 깜박이며
아리송한 표정을 짓다가
한참 지난 후에

그럼, 물소리 바람소리
모두 엄마나 가져 했다

날마다 뜨는 해
달마다 차오르다가 이지러지는 달
푸른 산 붉은 산
쉬지 않고 흐르는 강물
줄지도 넘치지도 않는 바다

그 후 아들은
산을 볼 때마다
심지어 가을 하늘을 바라보며
눈 내리는 창밖을 내다보며
엄마, 이거 엄마 다 가져

그렇게 한세상이 지났다

Part 6

Again in Spring

To birdsong,

my ears open

To cornelian cherry blossoms,

my eyes open

All things

open in this season—

But truly,

it is the heart

that must open

다시 봄에

새소리에
귀가 열리고
산수유에
눈이 열리고
모두
열리는 계절
정작
마음을 열어야지
.

Meeting

I come without an appointment
for I longed to see you
Though you are not here,
this heart that longs for you—
I carry it with me,
twice as full

만남

약속 없이 간다
만나고 싶어 왔으니
그대 없지만
그대 그리는 마음
두 배로
안고 간다

Greed

I don't think

I've ever truly

won a fight against this

No matter how many times

I strike it down,

it keeps rising

to try and defeat me

Day or night,

it charges at me—

a natural enemy

탐욕

이것과 싸워서
이겨본 적이
없는 것 같다
무찌르고 무찔러도
계속 일어나서
나를 이기려 한다
밤낮을 가리지 않고
달려드는 천적이다

The Fire of the Heart

Anger and discord
are fires within the heart
In those fires,
it's not just you
or just me
that burns—
it consumes
us both

마음의 불

분노와 불화는
마음속 불이다
그 불에는
너만 태우고
나만 타는 것이 아니라
너와 나
모두를 태운다

Life

A wave

is not just a wave

It wraps itself

in a thousand layers of foam,

becomes a thousand-fold surge—

and through the anguish of eternity,

it comes into being

인생

파도는
그냥 파도가 아니오
천 겹의 거품을 두르고
천 겹의 물결이 되어
영원을 고뇌하며
이루어지는 것이라오

Greetings for Friends

As spring returns,

flower buds form

on old branches—

a silent way

we ask

how each other has been

벗에게

새봄이 되어
묵은 가지에
꽃봉오리가 맺히는 것은
침묵으로 묻는
서로의 안부

After the Flowers Fell

When the flowers bloomed,
I didn't know they were flowers
Only after they fell
did I realize—
my whole life
had been a field of blossoms

꽃 지고 나서

꽃 필 때는
꽃인 줄 몰랐고
꽃 지고 나서
인생이 온통
꽃밭이었던 걸
알았다오

Farewell

You have returned to earth,
and I see a flower
blooming in my heart
This flower
has bloomed this year,
and will bloom again next year
As long as I can see the flowers,
they will bloom
year after year

고별

그대는 흙이 되었다
나는 마음에
피어난 꽃을 본다
이 꽃은
올해도 피었고
내년에도 필 것이다
내가 꽃을 볼 수 있는 한
꽃은 해마다
필 것이다

The Heart

If your heart is crooked,
the whole world
looks crooked
Even when slandered,
even when gossiped about—
if you keep your heart right,
it all simply passes by

마음

마음이 비뚤어져 있으면
세상이
비뚤어져 보인다
비방을 당해도
험담을 들어도
마음만 바로 하면
스쳐 지나가고 만다

That Is You

When I asked
how one should judge
another's small sin
to a grave sinner,
without hesitation
he said
"Punish it
severely and harshly"

그게 너다

중죄인에게
다른 이의
가벼운 죄를
어떻게 다스릴까 물었더니
서슴지 않고
중벌로 엄히 다스리란다

A Strange Road

Too late

to hold spring close,

too early

to embrace winter—

this life

at the edge of eighty—

though the road feels strange,

it is mine—

empty,

and waiting for me

낯선 길

봄을 품기에는
너무 늦었고
겨울을 품기는
이른 것 같은
인생 팔십 줄
낯선 길이지만
거기 내 길이
비어서 기다린다

Spring Is Brief

I shed winter
again and again—
yet it was still winter
I wrapped myself in spring
again and again—
yet spring was slow to come
To cast off
the past years,
I prostrate here
letting the years that walked over me
be carried away by the flowing water

봄은 짧고

겨울을 벗고
또 벗어도 겨울이었다
봄을 껴입고
또 껴입어도 봄은 더뎠다
지난 세월을
벗어버리자고
여기 이렇게 엎드려
나를 밟고 지나온 세월을
흐르는 물에 실려 보낸다

Despair

One who, no matter how much they have,
still wants more
One who, though it's rotting and reeks,
scrambles in hunger for more
Even with ten things in hand,
they do not turn away—
but reach once more
for yet another

절망

아무리 많아도
더 가지려는 사람
썩어서 냄새가 나는데도
부족해서 허덕이는 사람
열 개가 채워져도
돌아서지 않고
또 한 가지를
더 가지려는 사람

On Suffering

Even on a spring day
when flowers bloom,
the wind still blows

Even in the autumn sky,
dark clouds
can gather

고통에 대하여

꽃 피는
봄날에도
바람은 분다

가을 하늘에도
먹구름은
낀다

The Dream of AI

With just one app switched in,

we live long without illness,

cure obesity,

and have the child we want—

a son if we want a son,

a daughter if we want a daughter—

all in an instant

I invent an app

for beauty, kindness, and cleverness

In this world,

only tall, handsome, kind,

and smart people

will be born

Such a world—

Oh, how dreadful it would be

AI의 꿈

앱 하나 바꿔 끼우면
무병장수하고
비만도 해결하고
내가 원하는 아이도
아들이면 아들
딸이면 딸
일사천리라

잘생기고 착하고 머리 좋은
앱을 발명한다
이 세상에는 모두
키 크고 잘생기고 착하고
머리 좋은 사람만
태어나게 된다

그런 세상,
에구 끔찍스러워라

A Difference in Thought

Even living

under the same roof,

if our thoughts differ,

you are a distant

stranger to me

That difference in thought

is farther

than tens of thousands of miles

생각의 차이

한집에 살아도
생각이 다르면
멀리 있는
먼 사람이다
그 생각의 차이는
수수만리보다
더 멀다

My Home

The kitchen—
old-fashioned, simple bowls,
elegant, lovely teacups and spoons,
unpretentious yet graceful plates—
it is serene and warm

Then to the study—
writing implements worn by my hands,
dignified and deep
Books I miss, generous letters,
friendly photographs

Let's go to the dressing room
Spring, summer, autumn, winter—
clothes I wore through those seasons,
and there I meet my radiant youth
A proud young self,

with straight back and lifted chin,

nestles between the folds,

swaggering

I meet my fresh, young self again

The clear warmth of those days

grasps my hand deeply

As if hardened bones soften,

I'm escaping from time

The youth brimming with modest individuality,

whispers:

a stream of light

still pours into my soul

A hallucination

나의 집

부엌이다
예스럽고 담박한 그릇들
우아하고 예쁜 찻잔, 스푼
소탈하나 고운 접시들
그윽하고 따뜻하다

서재로 온다
손때 묻은 문방사우들
도도하고 도탑다
그리운 책들, 융숭한 편지들
정다운 사진들,

옷방으로 가자
봄, 여름, 가을, 겨울
이 옷들을 입고 생활하던
화사했던 청춘을 만난다
허리 굽지 않은 도도한 젊음이

거기 옷 갈피에 어깨를 맞대고
으스대듯 있다
풋풋했던 젊음을 만난다
그때의 맑았던 체온이
내 손을 깊게 잡는다
굳어진 뼈들이 물렁거리듯
세월을 벗어나고 있다
조촐한 개성이 넘치던 젊음이
아직도 내 영혼에 빛줄기가
쏟아지고 있다고 속삭인다

환청이다

A Ritual of Language: Of Words, By Words, For Words
— On the Poetry Collection *The Home of the Heart*

by Kim, Cho Hye

By Lee, Sung Chun

(Literary Critic, Professor at Kyung Hee University)

1. Kim, Cho Hye Is a Poet!

Kim, Cho Hye is a poet who has long carried within her the archetypal awareness of "poetry (詩) as a temple (寺) of words (言)." For her, poetry is the art of self-discipline carried out through language, and the aesthetics of spiritual awakening attained by means of words. She often emphasizes that "language is the total mode of human thought" and has, at every opportunity, insisted on the poetic consciousness and sense of mission that belong to the true poet, as well as the commitment to put that vision into aesthetic practice.

Her poetry collection, *The Home of the Heart*, is built upon this consciousness. It is a landscape of the heart that traces the journey of chaotic, worldly words returning to a realm of detachment. The collection depicts the quiet zone of spirit reached by pushing aside the noisy words of everyday life. This is why lines such as "With my right hand,/I reached for the worldly life/With my left hand,/I reached for a life beyond it/In such a fluster,/I ended up/grasping nothing at all" ("In a Fluster") appear so frequently in the book. The poems gather together words of enlightenment such as "It remains//in the hearts//of those//who are left behind" ("Next Life") and "Avalokiteshvara Bodhisattva// Even three thousand prostrations are//but a single lump//of burning tears" ("Eons").

Heidegger, in speaking of the essence of poetic creation, thoroughly examined the nature of language and its ontological role. He argued that language is the unique way in which human beings preserve the truth of Being, and that poetry—when grounded in the essence of language—reveals the original nature of existence. In this context, Heidegger invoked Holderlin, describing him as the "poet of poets" who awakened the people of a spiritually impoverished age.

This point, central to Heidegger's philosophy of art, is immensely useful for understanding Kim, Cho Hye's new poetry collection. If Heidegger defined the essence of poetry and poetic creation as the artistic act of elevating primordial thought into the realm of spiritual history, even in an age of deprivation, then in a similar vein Kim, Cho Hye declares that "A poet must hear/the sound of a heart/even from a taxidermied deer," and "from a wildflower,/A poet must awaken/to the truths of the universe" ("Poet"). Where Heidegger argued that a poet is the one who captures "what never disappears" even in a shattered world and binds it with language, Kim asserts with equal confidence that "poetry is humanity's primal essence," and that the path of the poet is "a path/where a pathless path/becomes a path" ("A Poet's Path" from *The Road to You*). In today's world—dominated by distorted and totalizing civilizational logic—Kim reminds the poets of our time of their responsibility, insisting that "a bell,/if not rung/is nothing more than/a lump of iron" ("To the Poet"). For her, the poet—especially the "poet of poets"—is someone who has been fated to embody the essence of poetry and poetic creation as a form of aesthetic action.

In this respect, Kim, Cho Hye is indeed a poet. She has always been one. This may sound curious, but the poetic world that Kim has built over sixty years can be summed up in a single sentence: Kim, Cho Hye is a poet! Since her debut in 1964— when she published "April," "In Front of the Door," and "The Road" in *Hyundae Munhak* through the recommendation of Midang Seo, Jeong Ju—she has maintained "the desire to become a poet without shame" (*Wandering Birds*, 1991). From her first collection *Wandering Star* (1984) to her recent *The Road to You* (2022), she has never strayed from this aspiration. Her confessions—such as "The shame I thought I had become immune to" (*Island*, 1987) keeps creeping in and "Like a habit, I hesitate every time I publish a new poetry collection" (*The Road to You*) — reveal the humility of a poet seeking to face the essence of poetry without sincerity.

Her poetic consciousness, which once declared "presence is absence/and absence is absence" ("Leper's Mask Dance·10"), reflected the image of a solitary self navigating the tragic age of loss and futility. In the 1980s, a time fraught with social and political unrest, her *Love Ritual* series offered solace to readers through a kind of poetic shamanism, embracing the world of "you" through the paradox of "I" in a grand epic of love. Even in times defined by "the double absence of deficiency" (as Heidegger described it), her poems, like the maternal figure in *Mother*(1988), became more earnest, heartfelt, and intellectually lucid. For Kim, love was another name for lyricism that feeds on suffering and sorrow, and poetic creation was a fated act of rigorous self-examination.

Thus, Kim's poetry is firmly rooted in her calling as a poet. Her work has always been constructed upon a deep sense of poetic responsibility. The emphatic statement—"What more do we need than poetry?" (*Love Ritual*, 2009)—resounds from "Literary Village" as evidence of that commitment. From the moment she lingered in "April", 'in front of the door" of poetry sixty years ago, she has never forgotten the role of "A poet is the one who cries/all the tears of the world" (*The Road to You*). Her hope— that "poems would serve as small lamps" (*Island*)— has never been lightly abandoned.

To her, poetry is a ritual of language meant to comfort and encourage human life. As she once wrote: "Poetry is human" (*The Path Taken on an Empty Boat*, 2009). Therefore, once again: Kim, Cho Hye is a poet. Her collection *The Home of the Heart* is another clear and resounding testament to this truth. In this new collection, Kim, Cho Hye contemplates the essence of poetry and poetic creation from multiple angles, giving form to the idea of "poetry (詩) as a temple (寺) of words (言)" in the sphere of everyday life. Through her words, her poetry, and her performance of language, she is once again conducting a ritual of words—by words, of words, and for words.

2. The Time of the "Rice Pot" and the Time of the "Flower Garden"

The etymological equation "poetry (詩) = the temple (寺) of words (言)" is a major premise for understanding Kim, Cho Hye's latest collection. In *The Home of the Heart*, she repeatedly emphasizes that poetry (詩) is, as the Chinese character suggests, a temple built from language—a space in which words are spiritually disciplined. The entire collection highlights poetry as an art of spiritual cultivation carried out through language, rooted in and dedicated to words.

I am nothing more/than a fifty-kilogram/rice pot/ When warm and full,/I spare no glance at my side/I'm just a rice pot/Yet to fill this mere/fifty-kilogram rice pot,/I have struggled/through an entire lifetime

—"Rice Pot" (complete)

Fearing my shameful self/might be seen by others,/
I spent a lifetime/covering my own eyes/I thought/if
I covered them,/all would be hidden

> —"A Lifetime" (complete)

They say/even stepping on/a single sprout/is a sin//
Then how many flowers/have I trampled/all this
time?

> —"Repentance" (complete)

Kim, Cho Hye's poetic discipline—language of,
by, and for words—is grounded in self-reflection.
True discipline is a function of the mind, and so
language-based cultivation begins in the arising
of mind, in the state of spiritual awakening. The
speaker's linguistic self-awareness thus involves
not only the purification of corrupted language,
but also the refinement of thought itself. Human
language and thought are inseparably bound. The
anthropological designation *Homo loquens*—"the
speaking human"—makes this truth explicit. To be
human is to speak and to think, and these functions

are eternally interdependent.

Accordingly, cultivation through language becomes a moral act that purifies the heart and trains thought in the direction of true insight. At the same time, it is a practice for the sake of language itself, elevating the words, thoughts, and awareness of others. This is why Kim's poetry — of, by, and for words — can be understood as an act of linguistic discipline. Similarly, it is also why her poetic practice constantly engages both the heart and the mind. Above all, it is because, as she writes, she is "always thinking" ("Poet's Note"), and because "poetry is human."

The poems "Rice Pot," "A Lifetime," and "Repentance" demonstrate clearly that her poetry arises from self-reflection. In each of these poems, the speaker — the self — is central. The speaker's heart drives the poem. "to fill this mere/fifty-kilogram rice pot,/I have struggled/through an entire lifetime" speaks to the anxious, hungry heart of "me." The shameful heart in "A Lifetime" that says "I spent a lifetime/covering my own eyes/I thought/if I covered them,/all would be hidden" reflects the poet's internal turmoil. The lament in "Repentance" that looks back on "how many flowers/have I trampled/all this time?" reveals a lyrical subject engaged in penitence. One particularly striking aspect of these three poems is that the speaker's heart is always set against the passage of time. Phrases such as "an entire lifetime," "a lifetime," and "all this time," highlight this shared foundation, and it is a deep characteristic of this collection as a whole. Clearly, Kim's poems are profoundly exposed to time.

Yet this does not mean her poems are hypersensitive to the passing years. Nor does it mean that she is intimidated by time's merciless nature. Rather, for Kim, Cho Hye, accumulated time functions as an absolute opportunity to reflect on her life and to articulate her confessions. It is a precious, irreplaceable moment for recognizing the truth of existence. Poems like "Hill after Hill," which calmly likens life's journey to crossing ridges, and "At Dusk," which expresses the feelings of existence that has entered the time zone of "before I knew it,/the light had dimmed—/it is already dusk," clearly reveal how the poet uses time gently and gracefully. "Spring Will Come" combines the poet's enlightenment with an experiential intelligence that "If you endure the cold season well,/spring will come." It reveals a time-consciousness shaped by both experience and awakening. In her poems, the passage of time does not merely point to physical aging or chronological progression. For her, physical age and scientific time are merely numbers.

Her poem "Just Because You're Old" articulates this clearly: "Just because you're old/doesn't mean you're wise/Just because you're old/doesn't mean you write good poetry/Just because you're old/ doesn't mean you're free of greed/Just because you're old/doesn't mean you have good character." This view strengthens the interpretation that she approaches time humbly and earnestly. In "Spring is Brief," she writes, "To cast off/the past years,/I prostrate here/letting the years that walked over me/ be carried away by the flowing water." In "Black Melancholy," she confesses, "I was only//caught by time,//but never//truly//caught time myself."

These expressions of humility, remorse, and awakening ultimately reveal time's blessing and the gift of words. The shame and repentance of "struggling to fill this rice pot," and the generous thoughts about "age" at "At Dusk" and "Hill after Hill" are the results of the language practice that Kim, Cho Hye's poetry has mastered. These self-reflective voices serve as the bedrock of her poetry. Even now, she continues to build her house of poetry with reflective language and a heart of realization. And through it all, time passes once more across the poet's frail shoulders.

Even the painful things/that seemed they would never be forgotten/even after a million, ten million eons/were all carried away by time

—"Time" (complete)

When the flowers bloomed,/I didn't know they were flowers/Only after they fell/did I realiz—/my whole life/had been a field of blossoms"

—"After the Flowers Fell" (complete)

When I think/that every cause/was my fault,/
forgiveness comes easily//But I forgive/only myself

—"Forgiveness" (complete)

One of the defining characteristics of Kim, Cho Hye's poetic method is her ability to summon transparent language and structure it in a concise form. The absence of excess in her lines, the frank and unadorned directness of her language, and the generous space she leaves between lines—all contribute to the enduring virtues of her poetry. The occasional use of conversational tones, confessional modes, and exclamatory endings complement this, resulting in a distinctly aesthetic formalism. In this way, her poetry preemptively distances itself from the discomforting tendencies of certain strains in the Korean literary scene—those marked by incoherent verbosity, communicative breakdowns, or despair-laden hysteria. It's fair to say that within her seemingly effortless language and the open gaps between lines lies Kim, Cho Hye's unique philosophy of language.

The poems above reflect, to a considerable degree, Kim, Cho Hye's formal approach. In "Time," we once again encounter her poetic conception of time. However, in this piece, time is not merely a marker of the passage of years or a repeated reference to moments like "dusk." Rather, time in "Time" plays a restorative role in life's wounds. The confessional tone in the lines, "Even the painful things/that seemed they would never be forgotten/even after a million, ten million eons/were all carried away by time" suggests that time, quietly and without fanfare, affirms the truth that "time heals all wounds."

How could this reversal phenomenon of time, that is, the time that flowed "mercilessly" ("Distance between Parents and Children") and brutally in Kim, Cho Hye's poetry, take on the role of healing? Across her collections, imagery of dusk and decay frequently appears, so how does time emerge here as a redemptive force? It may seem a trivial question, but it's not. Nor is it immature. For in this very vicinity resides Kim Cho-hye's flexible mindset that wholeheartedly affirms life "here and now," alongside a mature consciousness of time.

The following poems, "After the Flowers Fell" and "Forgiveness," clearly illustrate Kim, Cho Hye's current poetic worldview. They unfold with a gentle, confessional tone that gives the impression of the poet directly expressing her emotions. Yet the poetic messages feel assertive, owing to the speaker's use of definitive statements addressed to a listener. This also signifies that the poet's current emotional state has found a stable center of "calmness and composure" ("Hill after Hill"). This emotional grounding reflects her infinite affirmation of life and her ontological depth, an awareness of life's fundamental temporality. The reason "After the Flowers Fell" and "Forgiveness" convey such warm emotion and profound connection with life likely stems from this very foundation.

Now, the poet has come to know that every stage of life holds meaning in and of itself—as time spent in a "flower garden." Through accumulated experience, she breathes with time seasoned by existence and contemplates the meaning of the word forgiveness.

And so, she now says, "When the flowers bloomed,/ I didn't know they were flowers/Only after they fell/did I realize—/my whole life/had been a field of blossoms." And again: "When I think/that every cause/was my fault,/forgiveness comes easily."

3. A Ritual of Language That Feeds on Despair

The line, "When I was young,/youth was my excuse/Now that I am old,/oldness is/my big excuse" from the poem "Excuses," reflects a matured and seasoned state of mind. It is echoed by the refined thought found in, "Going together,/strength comes/ without gathering strength" ("Darkness"). Yet such understanding and composure are not obtained "just because you're old." Likewise, the ability to "hear a sound/that blossoms/into deeper stillness" ("The Sound of Stillness") or to realize that "The cold wind/makes flowers fall//The gentle wind/makes flowers bloom" ("To My Friend") is not something that comes automatically with age. For Kim, Cho Hye, it required sixty years of steadfast devotion to language—sixty years of poetic perseveration and disciplined words. With the unwavering resolve of a practitioner, she has walked the poet's path, one defined by the notion of "a path/where a pathless path/becomes a path."

I will not go/to his son's wedding/But isn't he your closest friend?/Ah, I no longer have/a child left to marry off

—"The Ways of the World" (Complete)

It's, a tiger/No, it's a leopard//It's, a goat/No, it's a sheep, I tell you//It's, a house/It's a residence//It's a person/No, it's a human being

—"Logic" (Complete)

One who, no matter how much they have,/still wants more/One who, though it's rotting and reeks,/scrambles in hunger for more/Even with ten things in hand,/they do not turn away—/but reach once more/for yet another

—"Despair" (Complete)

Still you say it is not enough/You have food to
eat,/a place to sleep,/and quietly,/unseen by anyone,/
flower seeds are blooming/toward you/Still,/what are
you lacking?

—"Contentment" (Complete)

It is a winding,/ever-turning road//a path layered/
fold upon fold//The road tells us/to live in the present,/
yet we stepped onto a path/that kills the present/in
order to live

—"Life in This World" (Complete)

Certainly, the path Kim, Cho Hye has walked as
a poet has not always been smooth. She confesses
at times to "forgive/only myself" ("Forgiveness") and
"Believing that/eternal time existed,/I walked and
walked/a long, distant road" ("In the Empty Sky"). She
had to pass through a "terrifying" world where
"A quiet/whispered word/can make a roar/more
frightening/than thunder and lightning" ("Slander"),
and confront the violence of a "finger-pointing"
world where "even without illness,/one will collapse

in pain" ("Finger-pointing"). She has encountered extreme internal contradictions, such as the "grave sinner" in "That Is You," and brushed past "crooked hearts" that are "of no use at all" ("Crooked Heart"). Along the way, she has resisted the temptation of "greed" "Day or night,/it charges at me — /a natural enemy" ("Greed") and endured the duplicity of people who, "In front, they smile,/behind, they sneer" ("Human Nature"). On one side of the poet's path lies the dismal landscape of selfishness, greed, slander, and baseless malice.

These poems stand as direct representation of such a landscape. In "The Ways of the World," the friendship between even the closest companions is reduced to a transaction governed by the logic of capital and exchange value. In "Logic," human beings, armed with arrogant reason, fall into blind opposition and descend into absurd argumentation. In "Despair," those who "no matter how much they have,/still wants more," live lives consumed by desire, always entangled in its chain reactions. In "Life in This World," we are told that, even as the road urges us to live in the present, we choose instead to kill it. When viewed together, these poems suggest a world in which the breakdown of logic and a loss of contentment lead inevitably to despair.

Throughout the collection, Kim, Cho Hye interweaves these signs of decay into the scenery of her poetic path, inserting the vulgarities of a materialistic society and the unadorned truths of a corrupt everyday life. She does not treat these as abstract criticisms but as the very structure of "the pathless path," recognizing them as the actual condition of lived despair.

> Darkness/where not even an inch ahead/can be seen//Yet within the darkness,/there is no darkness
>
> —"There Is Light" (Complete)

> You who have blinded my eyes/so I cannot see ahead,/do you say that/if I only open my heart,/being blind/is nothing at all?/Do you tell me to behold you/while deaf,/and while mute?
>
> —"Avatamsaka Sutra" (Complete)

The lives of those who have "stepped onto a path/that kills the present" are clearly marked by decline. In "Despair," the poet writes, "One who, no matter how much they have,/still wants more/One who, though it's rotting and reeks,/scrambles in hunger for more/Even with ten things in hand,/they do not turn away—/but reach once more/for yet another." These lives appear deeply precarious. As the poet notes, they are even "frightening." Or rather—perhaps more accurately—they are despairing.

Yet an even deeper despair afflicts our contemporary society: that we no longer recognize the erosion of our everyday ethics. The true tragedy of our modern condition lies in our forgetting how to despair. We, here and now, live in despair because we no longer know how to feel despair.

It may be in this very vicinity—within this ethical vacuum—that Kim, Cho Hye prepares her ritual of language: words of, by, and for language itself. For her, poetry is a spiritual language of witnessing a degraded world and awakening readers to seek "light" within the "darkness." It is the practical poetics of "Avatamsaka" where she insists that the hopeless path of a "pathless path" becomes a "path" when "I only open my heart."

Poor,/kind,/and diligent—//that's why//I like you

—"Disciple" (Complete)

To the great monk/I had long served,/I asked,//"Is there a next life?"//After a long silence,//"There is none."

—"There Is None" (Complete)

In a place so deeply, endlessly green,/there resides Venerable Jeongnyeom—/"Only when stillness is allowed to settle/can it truly be called stillness", —/ his teaching says//With palms together,/I receive it

—"Woljeongsa Temple" (Complete)

The most beautiful name/in this world/is Spring/ And there is another name/just like Spring//But that is a secret

—"Name" (Complete)

Kim, Cho Hye's poetry awakens readers to the fragile conditions of "life in this world," especially those navigating the spiritual poverty of the times. This is clearly evident throughout her collection *The Home of the Heart*. In "Money and Women," she satirizes the foolishness of adults by likening them to "fish." In "Sweet Trick," she "sweetly" exposes the hollowness of empty speech and the hypocrisy of those who speak it. And in "Greed," she personifies avarice itself, warning against humanity's moral collapse.

These poems, more often than not, challenge the exhaustion of contemporary language, which drifts unmoored from meaning, or they expose the perverse facade of modern capitalist systems. Particularly, they seek to involve the reader and form a shared recognition of "regret for our times"— within which the poet's intent is quietly embedded.

However, this does not mean that Kim, Cho Hye's poetry imposes its themes or pressures readers into awakening. Nor does it mirror the clumsy didacticism of outdated "enlightenment literature," which, captured by political zeal, fell into compulsive moral instruction. Rather, Kim Cho-hye believes such poetry has damaged the identity of lyric poetry and its singular emotional register. To her, that genre is no different from the noisy ritual of a false shaman. Her poetic judgment, honed through a lifetime of disciplined engagement with language, rejects excess and flood.

Kim's poems never resort to sensationalism or shock value. Instead, she favors the language of resonance and truth, as in her simple assertion, "A mountain is a mountain," "Water is water" ("I Don't Know"). She strives never to let go of a natural sensitivity and remembrance for life's essential values and the human condition.

The poverty described in "Disciple," presented as "Poor,/kind,/and diligent—//that's why//I like you," is likely a form of "voluntary poverty." Poverty, in itself, is rarely considered good or virtuous. Yet the poet declares, "that's why//I like you." This casual statement becomes possible only when poverty is chosen by a good life. Within this brief poem lies the poet's spring-like desire to affirm and bless the quietly good. Her language, like a folded secret, holds a protective charm against selfishness, greed, and deceit—recalling humanity's original kindness.

This language of protection also takes form in "There Is None" and "Woljeongsa Temple." Whether the "next life" exists or not, the poet suggests, depends on one's way of living "here and now." Thus, we must cast out anything that erodes life's original essence and strive to maintain stillness in mind and spirit. In "There Is None," this idea is conveyed through the "great monk" and his "long silence," expressing epistemological insight through a dialectic of being and non-being.

"Woljeongsa Temple" is a poem that "stillness is allowed to settle." Its language is clear, transparent, and serene. Like "There Is None," it allows no room for unnecessary commentary. What more could be added to such neat, restrained language? From this point on, we need only follow the spirit of the poem as it is. In "Woljeongsa Temple," the speaker receives the symbolic meaning of stillness "with palms together," bringing the vast and "deeply, endlessly green" "teachings" of Venerable Jeongnyeom and the language of truth into a world choked with noise. These two poems, gathered from Kim, Cho Hye's language of protection and purification, stand at the summit of her poetic ritual: words of, by, and for language itself. The poetic reverberations of "nonexistence" and "stillness" stimulate primordial thinking, offering our numb era a moment of deep reflection.

From this, one might arrive at a final understanding: Kim, Cho Hye's poetry feeds on "despair." Her poetics is a ritual where the language of protection and purification unfolds in full. Yet the music that emerges from this ritual is never mournful or desolate. For the words of enlightenment, always reaching toward origin, shine even in darkness. Because, as she writes, people with "The most beautiful name/in this world" "just like Spring" live here. Just like the earlier poems that sustained her through suffering, pain, and grief. Just like Holderlin, the "poet among poets" who lived through a spiritually destitute age.

4. The Poetics of "Yes, Yes"

With her sixtieth year as a poet, Kim, Cho Hye completed a full circle in her collection *The Home of the Heart*. This is not simply recalling her age within the sexagenary cycle. In fact, as she herself says with characteristic candor, "Just because you're old/doesn't mean you write good poetry." Rather, in *The Home of the Heart*, Kim fluently and assuredly reanimates the genre-defining concept that "poetry (詩) = the temple (寺) of words (言)," giving it new life through her seasoned poetic philosophy.

What can poetry offer in an age of scarcity? What must the language of lyricism do? Kim continues to pose these questions and ponder them seriously. She thinks that "Even a small Blemish/is still a blemish" ("Blemish"), and that "With one pillar/you cannot build a house" ("With Only One"), and thinks of the round motherhood that "love/cannot overcome/a mother" ("Love"). She remembers the human effort and passion of painter-scholar Chusa Kim, Jeong Hui who "wore holes/into ten inkstones" ("Blossoms") worries about people who "devour/themselves to ruin" ("Oh, Human"), and agonizes that "enlightenment/is too cruel/a reverence" ("Enlightenment"). She reflects on the poem "Life's Journey" with its sweeping vision, and critiques political figures in "Migratory Bird," while quietly contemplating the strangeness of turning eighty in "A Strange Road." Sometimes, she recalls "a thousand strands of memory" "From the kimchi soup//I had for dinner," ("Thinking of Home"), or sinks into the thought that "Any place where you can recall/your parents and siblings/is a hometown" ("Hometown").

Thus, the poet says "I am always thinking." "So I read, and I write." ("Poet's Note"). Through this process, her poems critique the vulgarity of low-brow capitalism and the overgrown desires that saturate human behavior. Her language reflects on the lives of modern people who have forgotten life's original essence, and her poetry encourages reflection on human truth and the secrets of life. Through the disciplined practice of language, she stirs the dormant capacity for fundamental thought in those suffering from conceptual paralysis.

In *The Home of the Heart*, we meet the mother who gave her nothing but the thin broth of watery spinach soup ("Spinach Soup"), the good and diligent disciple who chooses voluntary poverty ("Disciple"), and the great monk at Woljeongsa Temple who dwells in perfect stillness. All these figures share a common spiritual space. Also residing there are the unnamed, spring-like beings who have not yet revealed themselves — beings whom the poet regards as transcendents living within the secular world. Perhaps this is why the book is able to hold a balance of sharp critical spirit, warm satire, and playful humor. *The Home of the Heart* is, ultimately, a ritual of language — of, by, and for words — that is never overwrought or pitiful.

The child monk statue/sent by artist Lee, Sang Ho from Gwangju/keeps nodding all day/and taps his moktak/whenever there is light/Even to the rambling sophistry without reason,/Yes, yes, you are right/ Even to the vile acts that evade the truth,/Yes, yes,

you are right/Yes, yes, only you are right/Always,
you are right/The child monk is on my side/And I am
on the child monk's side. too

—"Yes, Yes" (Complete)

At this point in the commentary, one might wish to return a beautiful poem to this poet of sixty years. Perhaps a poem like "Yes, Yes," which could well be hung on the door of her poetic house. A poem where the seasoned poet's generous, radiant, and kind heart is fully revealed. A poem that affirms the closed circle of the proposition: Kim, Cho Hye is a poet. She has always been a poet.

And so, like the child monk who gently nods his head while tapping the wooden moktak, I too am on the poet's side. I stand with Kim, Cho Hye, who has never once turned away from the essence of poetry and poetic creation.

So, oh poet, please never lay down your mantle for all eternity!

Introduction for International Readers

It seems important to try to live life without regrets, but sometimes life makes that aspiration difficult to realize. When I encountered the poetry of Kim, Cho Hye, I was surprised to discover that my initial emotional reaction was regret, but of an unexpected origin: Regret that I cannot read or understand Korean. The translations of her work into this first English volume, as you'll see, are magnificent. But their spare beauty made me wonder, and wish that I could experience firsthand, her language in the original.

The regret passed quickly, thanks to Kim, Tae

Kyun and his son, Kim, Yoon Shik, whose glorious English-language translation has given poetry lovers around the world a gift with this new volume. A sip of ambrosia isn't a cup, but it's still ambrosia. And even in English, the deep well of compassion from which Ms. Kim draws is in abundant evidence.

No poet wants to be pigeonholed. When someone calls Mary Oliver a "nature poet," I bridle, since her work—though often set outdoors—contains so much more than trees, rivers, birds. But I think, I hope, that if I call Ms. Kim a poet of human connection, she would not be insulted, since, to borrow a phrase from another poet, Ms. Kim's human connections "contain multitudes." A mother to her son about what endures ("To My Son"); despair and frustration on reflecting on one's own life journey (in her anguished "Rice Pot"), alienation that can arise even between those who love each other ("A Difference in Thought") or sepia-toned memory ("In Life"); our older selves reflecting wisdom to our younger ones over life's span ("Hill after Hill"); offerings of compassion's salve to all those turning on Samsara's wheel (too many to list, but don't miss "Who Is It"); wherever you look in this new volume, you'll find the work of a poet of human connection, a poet who draws fellow sufferers into a great, warm embrace.

W.H. Auden's injunction, "love your crooked neighbor/with your crooked heart" came to mind often as I read Ms. Kim's poems. But more important than what came to mind was what my crooked heart felt as I read this volume. Clearly enough, it was love.

My connection to this work comes through Kim, Tae Kyun, a practicing Buddhist and a gorgeous poet in his own right. Though neither he nor I are scholars of the humanities, we both are surgeons, and as such, we may know a bit more about death than do some people. I don't mean this in any dark way; it's the fact of death that gives human life its beauty. This motif, as much as love and connection, recurs in Ms. Kim's work, perhaps no more clearly than in her terse but luminous poem "Next Life," which shares an essential truth about life's end for all of us, a truth well worth considering as we grow older:

It remains

in the hearts

of those

who are left behind

I believe "Next Life" is TK's favorite in this volume. I tried to pick a favorite but couldn't. There are just too many good ones, as you will soon see.

Seth S. Leopold, MD
Seattle, WA, USA

국제 독자를 위하여

후회 없는 삶을 살아가는 것이 중요하다는 말은 흔히 들리지만, 인생은 때때로 그 뜻을 실현하기 어렵게 만듭니다. 김초혜 시인의 시를 처음 접했을 때, 제게 가장 먼저 찾아온 감정은 뜻밖에도 후회였습니다. 그것은 시인의 시어를 온전히 이해할 만큼 한국어를 알지 못한다는 후회였습니다.

이 첫 번째 영문 시집에 실린 번역들은 참으로 탁월합니다. 그러나 그 절제된 아름다움 속에서 저는 원문이 지닌 언어의 숨결을 직접 느껴보고 싶다는 아쉬움을 금할 수 없었습니다.

다행히 그 후회는 오래가지 않았습니다. 김태균 선생님과 그의 아들 김윤식 님의 훌륭한 번역 덕분에, 이제 전 세계의 시 애호가들이 이 시집을 통해 귀한 선물을 받게 되었기 때문입니다. 신들의 음료인 암브로시아를 한 모금만 마신다 해도 그것이 여전히 암브로시아이듯, 영어로 옮겨진 이 시집에서도 김초혜 시인의 깊은 연민과 사랑의 샘은 풍성히 흘러나옵니다.

어느 시인도 자신이 한 범주로 규정되는 것을 원하지 않습니다. 누군가가 메리 올리버를 "자연 시인"이라 부를 때마다 저는 불편함을 느낍니다. 그녀의 시가 종종 자연을 배경으로 하긴 하지만, 그 안에는 나무와 새, 강물 이상의 세계가 담겨 있기 때문입니다.

그렇기에 감히 말씀드리자면, 저는 김초혜 시인을 "인간의 연결을 노래하는 시인"이라 부르고 싶습니다. 다른 시인의 말을 빌리자면, 그녀의 인간적 연결은 "무수한 세계를 품고" 있습니다.

아들에게 전하는 사랑과 인내의 메시지(「아들에게」), 자신의 삶을 되돌아보며 토로하는 절망과 분노(「밥통」), 사랑하는 이들 사이조차 스며드는 거리감(「생각의 차이」), 빛바랜 추억 속의 온기(「삶 속에서」), 세월을 건너 젊은 날의 자신에게 건네는 지혜(「고개 고개 넘어」), 윤회의 수레바퀴 위에 서 있는 모든 이에게 바치는 연민의 위로(「누구인가요」를 비롯한 다수의 시). 이 한 권의 시집 어디를 펼쳐보아도, 우리는 인간의 고통을 따뜻하게 끌

어안는 시인의 품을 만나게 됩니다.

"애환 속에 사는 이웃을, 애환을 경험한 마음으로 사랑하라." 이 말이 이 시집을 읽는 동안 제 마음속에 오래 머물렀습니다. 그러나 더 중요한 것은, 그 문장을 떠올릴 때 제 안에서 일어난 감정이었습니다. 그 감정은 다름 아닌 사랑이었습니다.

이 시집과의 인연은 김태균 선생님을 통해 맺어졌습니다. 그는 불교 수행자이자, 동시에 자신만의 시 세계를 지닌 아름다운 시인이기도 합니다.

우리 둘 다 인문학자는 아니지만, 의사이자 외과의로 살아오며 누구보다 죽음의 실체를 가까이에서 보아온 사람들입니다. 그것은 어두운 의미가 아닙니다. 오히려 죽음이 존재하기에 삶이 더욱 빛난다는 뜻입니다. 이 주제는 사랑과 연결만큼이나 김초혜 시인의 시에 자주 등장하며, 그 정수는 간결하면서도 찬란한 시 「내생」에 잘 드러납니다. 이 시는 우리 모두가 언젠가 맞이할 생의 끝에 관한 진실을 잔잔히 일깨워 줍니다.

「내생」

남은

사람들의

가슴에

있다

「내생」이 김태균 선생님께서 가장 아끼는 작품이라 들었습니다. 저도 가장 마음에 드는 한 편으로 고르고자 하였으나 하지 못했습니다. 마음을 울리는 시가 너무 많기 때문입니다.

세스 레오폴드, 의학박사
미국 시애틀에서

Celebrating the Publication of Kim, Cho Hye's Poetry Collection (Korean–English Edition)

There are poems that transcend the boundaries of literature. They become acts of spiritual cultivation—traces of an inner journey honed with time and sincerity. The verses of Kim, Cho Hye composed in a language both resolute and compassionate, invite us to pause, reflect, and return to the essence of our lives.

In her restrained words lie profound resonance, a gaze that is humble yet steadfast. Her poetry—marked by honesty and constancy—reveals her unwavering commitment not only as a poet, but also as a wife, mother, grandmother, and member of this world. Above all, she holds firm to the belief that one must live one's own life righteously.

Though I lack formal expertise in poetry or English literature, I find myself making a quiet vow each time I read her work — to live this day, and my life, in the right way.

With this collection published in both English and Korean, I am truly delighted that many people around the world will be able to share the inspiration and resolve I have received.

I offer my heartfelt thanks for Ms. Kim's steadfast journey and words, and I sincerely hope that this publication will be warmly welcomed by many.

Kim, Tae Kyun
TK Life Care Director

김초혜 시집 한영판 발간을 축하하며

문학의 경계를 넘어서는 시가 있습니다.

그것들은 한 사람의 내면이 세월과 성찰로 다듬어낸 수행의 자취가 되어, 읽는 이로 하여금 잠시 멈추어 서서 자신의 삶을 되돌아보게 합니다.

김초혜 시인의 시편들이 바로 그러합니다.

단단하면서도 자비로운 언어로 엮인 그녀의 시는

우리에게 멈춤과 사유의 시간을 건네며

삶의 본질로 되돌아가게 합니다.

절제된 말 속에 깃든 울림, 겸허하면서도 흔들림 없는 시선.

그것은 시인으로서의 진정성일 뿐 아니라, 아내로서, 어머니로서, 할머니로서, 그리고 이 세상 한 구성원으로서의 변함없는 자세를 보여줍니다.

무엇보다 그녀의 시에는

"자신의 삶을 바르게 살아야 한다"는 믿음이 깊이 흐르고 있습니다.

저는 시나 영문학의 전문가는 아니지만, 그녀의 시를 읽을 때마다 마음속으로 다짐합니다.

오늘 하루를, 그리고 내 삶을 바르게 살아가겠노라고.

이번 시집이 한글과 영어로 함께 세상에 나와 전 세계의 많은 이들이 시인께서 전해 주신 감동과 다짐을 함께 나눌 수 있게 된 것을 진심으로 기쁘게 생각합니다.

김초혜 시인의 한결같은 걸음과 언어에 깊이 감사드리며,

이 시집이 많은 이들의 마음속에 따뜻이 받아들여지기를 바랍니다.

김태균
TK Life Care 대표원장

It is a profound honor to celebrate the publication of Kim, Cho Hye's poetry collection, *The Home of the Heart*. Having had the privilege of co-translating these poems alongside my father, Kim, Tae Kyun, this project became far more than an act of translation. It was a journey of shared discovery that deepened not only my understanding of language but also my connection to the poet herself and the world she has so eloquently lived through.

Born in 1943, Kim, Cho Hye represents a generation that witnessed the turbulence and transformation of post-war Korea. Yet the enduring power of her poetry lies in its universality. Beneath her quiet tone runs an unflinching honesty, a deeply human voice that confronts pain, tenderness, frustration, and anger, alongside love and compassion. Though I am of a different generation, I found her words strikingly resonant. They speak to what is timeless in us: our longing for meaning, connection, and grace amid change.

Her poems reveal the full spectrum of the human heart, sorrow and weariness, but also gentleness, devotion, and love for life in all its imperfection. What moves me most is how her work embraces contradiction. It allows space for disillusionment without bitterness, for grief that coexists with gratitude.

At its core, *The Home of the Heart* is an act of love for humanity, for imperfection, and for the world as it is. It offers consolation and quiet strength to readers at every stage of life. I am deeply grateful to have helped bring her voice to a wider audience, and I hope this collection will be read not only as poetry, but as a testament to the grace and courage of living.

Kim, Yoon Shik

Translator

김초혜 시인의 시집 『마음의 집』 영문판 출간을 진심으로 축하드립니다.

이번 번역 작업은 단순한 언어의 옮김을 넘어선, 아버지 김태균 선생님과 함께한 깊은 배움의 여정이었습니다. 그 과정에서 저는 언어에 대한 이해뿐 아니라, 시인이 살아온 세상과 그녀의 마음에 더 가까이 다가갈 수 있었습니다.

1943년에 태어난 김초혜 시인은 전후 한국의 격동과 변화를 온몸으로 겪어낸 세대를 대표합니다. 그러나 그녀의 시가 지닌 힘은 시대를 초월한 보편성에 있습니다. 담담한 어조 속에서도 결코 피하지 않는 정직함, 그리고 꾸밈이나 가식 없이 고통과 연민, 좌절과 분노, 그리고 사랑과 자비를 함께 마주하는 인간적인 목소리가 흐르고 있습니다. 비록 저는 다른 세대에 속하지만, 시인의 언어는 제 마음에도 깊이 닿았습니다. 그것은 우리가 모두 공유하는, 변화 속에서도 의미와 연결, 그리고 품위를 찾고자 하는 인간의 본질적인 갈망을 이야기하고 있기 때문입니다.

그녀의 시는 인간의 마음을 이루는 전 영역을 보여줍니다. 슬픔과 피로, 그러나 동시에 온유함과 헌신, 불완전한 삶에 대한 깊은 사랑이 함께 존재합니다. 무엇보다 인상적인 점은 그녀의 시가 삶의 모순을 포용한다는 것입니다. 좌절 속에서도 씁쓸함이 없고, 슬픔 속에서도 감사가 깃들어 있습니다.

『마음의 집』은 결국 인간과 세상, 그리고 불완전함을 향한 사랑의 기록입니다. 이 시집은 모든 세대의 독자들에게 위로와 조용한 힘을 건넵니다. 시인의 목소리를 더 넓은 세계에 전할 수 있다는 사실에 깊이 감사드리며, 이 작품이 단순한 시집을 넘어, 살아가는 일의 은혜와 용기를 증언하는 책으로 오래도록 읽히기를 바랍니다.

김윤식
옮긴이

The Home of the Heart

제1판 1쇄 2025년 11월 24일

지은이 | 김초혜
옮긴이 | 김태균 · 김윤식
펴낸이 | 송영석

편집장 | 박신애
기획편집 | 최예은 · 이나연
디자인 | 박윤정 · 유보람
마케팅 | 김유종 · 한승민
관리 | 송우석 · 전지연 · 채경민

펴낸곳 | (株)해냄출판사
등록번호 | 제10-229호
등록일자 | 1988년 5월 11일(설립일자 | 1983년 6월 24일)

04042 서울시 마포구 잔다리로 30 해냄빌딩 5 · 6층
대표전화 | 326-1600 **팩스** | 326-1624
홈페이지 | www.hainaim.com

ISBN 979-11-6714-137-8

파본은 본사나 구입하신 서점에서 교환하여 드립니다.